SPECIAL FAMILY EDITION

The Quiet Little Woman

Louisa May Alcott

Illustrations by C. Michael Dudash

HONOR
BOOKS

Tulsa, Oklahoma

The Quiet Little Woman, gift edition

ISBN 1-56292-771-X
Copyright©2000 by Stephen W. Hines

Published by Honor Books
P.O. Box 55388
Tulsa, Oklahoma 74155

Book design by Koechel Peterson & Associates
Illustrations by C. Michael Dudash

A GIFT OF LOVE

"Best wishes for the success of Little Things and its brave young proprietors."

These words were written by Louisa May Alcott to Carrie, Maggie, Nellie, Emma, and Helen Lukens on the founding of their home-produced magazine.

Miss Alcott wrote many encouraging letters to the Lukens girls and even sent them her picture. Her kind attention to these five young women is all the more remarkable for the fact that she was in the midst of a very busy writing career that sometimes put great stress on her physically. Alcott's health had been poor since she served as a nurse during the Civil War. At a time when her stories were bringing several hundred dollars apiece— a large sum in those days—she sent along this beautiful tale for *Little Things*, "for love—not for money" as she put it.

This then is how the story "Patty's Place" ("The Quiet Little Woman") came to be. It was, as Miss Alcott said, "a gift of love." You, too, will cherish this offering from one of the world's great writers, just as the Lukens girls did more than one hundred years ago.

Stephen W. Hines

*P*ATTY STOOD AT THE WINDOW LOOKING THOUGHTFULLY DOWN AT A GROUP OF GIRLS PLAYING IN THE YARD BELOW. ALL WORE BROWN GOWNS WITH BLUE APRONS, AND ALL WERE ORPHANS LIKE HERSELF. SOME WERE PRETTY AND SOME PLAIN, SOME ROSY AND GAY, SOME PALE AND FEEBLE.

"Oh, if someone would only come and take me away! I'm so tired of living here and I don't think I can bear it much longer."

Poor Patty might well wish for a change; she had been in the orphanage ever since she could remember. And though everyone was very kind to her, she was heartily tired of the place and longed to find a home.

*A*t the orphanage, the children were taught and cared for until they were old enough to help themselves; then they were adopted or went to work as servants. Now and then, some forlorn child was claimed by family. And once, the relatives of a little girl named Katy proved to be rich and generous people, who came for her in a fine carriage, treated all the other girls in honor of the happy day, and from time to time, let Katy visit them with arms full of gifts for her former playmates and friends.

Katy's situation made a great stir in the orphanage, and the children never tired of talking about it and telling it to newcomers as a sort of modern day fairy tale. But by and by, Katy ceased to come, and gradually new girls took the places of those who had left. Eventually, Katy's good fortune was forgotten by all but Patty. To her, it remained a splendid possibility.

But year after year, no one came for Patty.

*P*atty's pale face, short figure with one shoulder higher than the other, and shy ways limited her opportunities. She was not ill now, but looked so, and was a sober, quiet little woman at the age of thirteen.

The good matron often recommended Patty as a neat, capable, and gentle little person; but no one seemed to want her. After every failure, her heart grew heavier and her face sadder, for the thought of spending the rest of her life there in the orphanage was unbearable.

No one guessed what a world of hopes and thoughts and feelings lay hidden beneath that blue pinafore, what dreams this solitary child enjoyed, or what a hungry, aspiring young soul lived in her crooked little body. But God knew, and when the time came, He remembered Patty and sent her the help she so desperately needed. . . .

As Patty said aloud with a great sigh, "I don't think I can bear it any longer!" a hand touched her shoulder and a voice said gently—

"Bear what, my child?"

The touch was so light and the voice so kind that Patty answered before she had time to feel shy.

"Living here, ma'am, and never being chosen as the other girls are."

"Tell me all about it, dear. I'm waiting for my sister, Mrs. Murray. I'm Miss Jane Jenson, but you can call me Aunt Jane. I'd like to hear your troubles," the kindly woman said, sitting down in the window seat and drawing Patty beside her. She was a gray-haired woman dressed in plain black, but her eyes were so cheerful and her voice so soothing that Patty felt at ease in a minute and nestled up to her as she shared her little woes in a few simple words.

As Patty spoke, Aunt Jane noted the sadness in the young girl's face, and tried to brighten her mood. Then with a kiss that won Patty's heart, Aunt Jane went away, casting more than one look of pity at the small figure sitting in the window seat.

For a week after this, Patty went about her work with a sad face, and all her daydreams were of living with Aunt Jane in the country.

*M*onday afternoon, as Patty stood sprinkling clothes for ironing, one of the girls burst in, saying all in a breath—

"Patty! Someone has come for you at last. It's Mrs. Murray, the one who took Lizzy. Mrs. Murray says that Lizzy is a lazy girl and will not do at all. She is insisting that you must come in her place. Do hurry, and don't stand staring at me that way."

"It can't be me—no one ever wants me— it's some mistake—"stammered Patty. She was so startled and excited that she did not know what to say or do.

"It's no mistake," the girl insisted. "The matron says you are to come right up. Go along—I'll finish here. I'm so glad you have your chance at last!"And with a good-natured hug, the girl pushed Patty out of the kitchen.

In a few minutes, Patty came flying back in a twitter of delight to report that she was leaving at once and must say goodbye. Everyone was pleased, and when the flurry was over, the carriage drove away with the happiest little girl you have ever seen riding inside, for at last someone did want her. Patty had found a place.

During the first year Patty lived with the Murrays, they found her to be industrious, docile, and faithful—and yet she was not happy and had not found with them all she expected. They were kind to her, providing plenty of food and not too much work. They clothed her comfortably, let her go to church, and did not scold her very often.

But no one showed love to her, no one praised her efforts, no one seemed to think that she had any hope or wish beyond her daily work; and no one saw in the shy, quiet little maiden a lonely, tenderhearted girl longing for a crumb of the love so freely given to the children of the home.

The master and his oldest son were busy caring for the family's large farm, and Mrs. Murray was a brisk, smart housewife who "flew 'round" herself and expected others to do the same. Pretty Ella, the daughter, was about Patty's age and busy with her school, her little pleasures, and all the bright plans young girls love and live for. Two or three small lads, one of them lame, rioted about the house making much work and doing very little.

"*S*he's only a servant, a charity girl who works for her board and wears my old clothes. She's good enough in her place, but of course she can't expect to be like one of us," Ella once said to a young friend—and Patty heard her.

"Only a servant. . . ." That was the hard part, and it never occurred to anyone to make it softer. So Patty plodded on, still hoping and dreaming about friends and fortune.

But Mrs. Murray's sister, Aunt Jane Jenson, had never forgotten about Patty or the few words they shared as they sat on the windowseat. Even though she lived twenty miles away and seldom came to the farm, Aunt Jane wrote to the family once a month and never failed to include a little note to Patty. The lonely girl always replied, pouring out her heart to this one friend who sent her encouraging words and cheered her with praise now and then.

This was Patty's anchor in her little sea of troubles, and she clung to it, hoping for the day when she had earned such a beautiful reward that she would be allowed to go and live with Aunt Jane.

Christmas was coming and the family was filled with great anticipation, for they intended to spend the day at Aunt Jane's and bring her home for dinner and a dance the next day. For a week beforehand, Mrs. Murray flew 'round with more than her accustomed speed, and Patty trotted about from morning till night, lending a hand to all the most disagreeable jobs.

When everything was done at last, Mrs. Murray declared that she would drop if she had another thing to do but go to Jane's and rest.

Patty had lived on the hope of going with them, but nothing was said about it. At last, they all trooped gaily away, leaving her to take care of the house and see that the cat did not touch one of the dozen pies carefully stored in the pantry.

Patty kept up bravely until they were gone, then she sat down like Cinderella, and cried and cried until she could cry no more. The shower of tears did her good, and she went about her work with a meek, patient face that would have touched a heart of stone.

When Aunt Jane welcomed the family, her first word, as she emerged from the chaos of small
boys' arms and legs, was "Why, where is Patty?"

"At home, of course; where else would she be?" answered Mrs. Murray.

"Here with you. I said 'all come' in my letter; didn't you understand it?"

Aunt Jane knit her brows and looked vexed, and Ella laughed at the idea of a servant girl going on
holiday with the family.

They had a capital time, and no one observed that Aunty, now and then, directed the conversation to Patty by asking a question about her or picking up on every little hint dropped by the boys concerning her patience and kindness.

At last, Mrs. Murray said, as she sat resting with a cushion at her back, a stool at her feet, and a cup of tea steaming deliciously under her nose, "I've entire confidence in Patty. I have no doubt that she is equal to taking care of the house for a week, if need be. On the whole, Jane, I consider her a pretty promising girl. She isn't very quick, but she is faithful, steady, and honest as daylight."

"*S*he's first rate and takes care of me better than anyone else," said Harry, the lame boy, with sudden warmth. Patty had quite won his selfish little heart by many services.

"She'll make Mother a nice helper as she grows up, and I consider it a good speculation. In four years, she'll be eighteen, and if she goes on doing so well, I won't begrudge her wages," added Mr. Murray, who sat nearby with a small son on each knee.

"She'd be quite pretty if she were straight and plump and jolly. But she is as sober as a deacon, and when her work is done, she sits in a corner watching us with big eyes, as shy and mute as a mouse," said Ned, the big brother, lounging on the sofa.

"A dull, steady-going girl, suited for a servant and no more," concluded Mrs. Murray, setting down her cup as if the subject were closed.

"You are quite mistaken, and I'll prove it!" Aunt Jane announced, jumping up so energetically that the boys laughed and the elders looked annoyed. Pulling out a portfolio, she untied a little bundle of letters, saying impressively—

"Now listen, all of you, and see what has been going on with Patty this year."

Then Miss Jane read the little letters that Patty had written to her, one by one, and it was curious to see how the faces of the listeners first grew attentive and finally filled with interest and respect and something very much like affection.

As they grew to know Patty as she was, each felt sorry that he or she had not found her out before. They continued to discuss her kind words until quite an enthusiastic state of feeling set in and Patty was in danger of being killed with kindness.

They laid many nice little plans to surprise Patty, and each privately resolved not only to give her a Christmas gift but also to do the better thing by bringing her fully into the family during the year ahead.

All the way home, they talked over their various projects, and the boys kept bouncing into the seat with Aunt Jane to ask advice about their funny ideas.

"It must have been rather lonesome for the poor little soul all day. I declare, I wish we'd taken her along!" said Mrs. Murray, as they approached the house through the softly falling snow.

"I hope the child isn't sick or scared. It's two hours later than I expected to be home," added Mr. Murray, stepping up to peep in at the kitchen window, for no one came to open the door and no light but the blaze of the fire shone out.

"Come softly and look in," he whispered, beckoning to the rest. "It's a pretty little sight even if it is in a kitchen."

Quietly creeping to the two low windows, they all looked in, and no one said a word, for the lonely little figure was both pretty and pathetic when they remembered the letters lately read. Patty lay flat on the old rug, fast asleep with one arm pillowed under her head. In the other arm lay Puss in a cozy bunch, as if she had crept there to be sociable since there was no one else to share Patty's long vigil. A row of slippers, large and small, stood warming on the hearth, two little nightgowns hung over a chair, the teapot stood in a warm nook, and through the open door, they could see the lamp burning brightly in the sitting room, the table ready, and all things in order.

"Faithful little creature! She's thought of every blessed thing," cried Mrs. Murray, heading for the door.

"And look there," whispered Bob, pointing to the poor little gifts half tumbling out of Patty's apron. No one laughed at the presents, but gazed at them with looks of tender pity.

No one exactly knew how to awaken the sleeper, for she was something more than a servant in their eyes now. Aunt Jane settled the matter by stooping down and taking Patty in her arms. The big eyes opened at once and stared up at the face above. Then a smile so bright, so glad, shone all over the child's face as she clung to Aunt Jane, crying joyously—

"Is it really you? I was so afraid you wouldn't come that I cried myself to sleep."

Never before had any of them seen such love and happiness in Patty's face, heard such a glad, tender sound in her voice, or guessed what an ardent soul dwelt in her quiet body.

Soon the family went off to bed, and Patty was surprised by the kind goodnights everyone sent her way. But she thought no more of it than to feel that Aunt Jane brought a warmer atmosphere to the home.

$\mathcal{P}$atty's surprise began early the next day, for the first thing she saw upon opening her eyes was a pair of new stockings crammed full of gifts hanging at the foot of her bed and several parcels lying on the table.

They do care for me after all, and I never will complain again, she thought. Such a happy child was she that when she tried to say her prayers, she couldn't find words beautiful enough to express her gratitude for so much kindness.

It was the merriest Christmas ever, and when the bountiful dinner was spread and Patty stood

ready to wait, you can imagine her feelings as Mr. Murray pointed to a seat near Aunt Jane and said

in a fatherly tone that made his gruff voice sweet—

"Sit down and enjoy it with us, my girl; nobody has more right to it, and we are all one family today."

More surprises came that evening. When she went to put on her clean calico smock, she found a

pretty blue dress and white apron laid ready on her bed along with a note that read, "With Ella's love."

*W*hen everyone was gone, the tired children asleep, and the elders on their way up to bed, Mrs. Murray suddenly remembered she had not covered the kitchen fire. Aunt Jane said she would do it, and went down so softly that she did not disturb faithful Patty, who had also gone to see that all was safe.

Aunt Jane stopped to watch the little figure standing on the hearth alone, looking into the embers with thought-ful eyes. If Patty could have seen her future there, she would have found a long life spent in glad service to those she loved and who loved her. Not a splendid future, but a useful, happy one—"only a servant," perhaps, yet a good and faithful woman, blessed with the confidence, respect, and affection of those who knew her genuine worth.

As a smile broke over Patty's face, Aunt Jane said with an arm round the little blue-gowned figure—

"What are you dreaming and smiling about, deary? The friends that are to come for you someday, with a fine fortune in their pockets?"

"No ma'am, I feel as if I've found my folks. I don't want any finer fortune than the love they've given me today. I'm trying to think how I can deserve it and smiling because it's so beautiful and I'm so happy," answered Patty, looking up at her first friend with full eyes and a glad glance that made her lovely.

The End